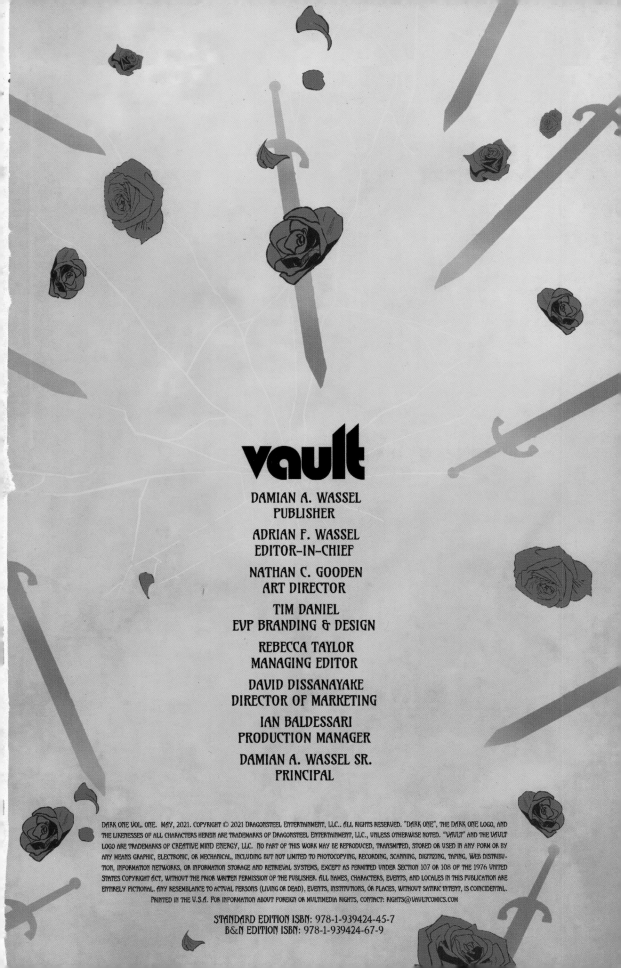

vault

DAMIAN A. WASSEL
PUBLISHER

ADRIAN F. WASSEL
EDITOR-IN-CHIEF

NATHAN C. GOODEN
ART DIRECTOR

TIM DANIEL
EVP BRANDING & DESIGN

REBECCA TAYLOR
MANAGING EDITOR

DAVID DISSANAYAKE
DIRECTOR OF MARKETING

IAN BALDESSARI
PRODUCTION MANAGER

DAMIAN A. WASSEL SR.
PRINCIPAL

STANDARD EDITION ISBN: 978-1-939424-45-7
B&N EDITION ISBN: 978-1-939424-67-9

CREATED & STORY BY
BRANDON SANDERSON

WRITTEN BY
JACKSON LANZING & COLLIN KELLY

DRAWN BY
NATHAN GOODEN

COLORED BY
KURT MICHAEL RUSSELL

LETTERED BY
ANDWORLD DESIGN

BRANDON SANDERSON'S
DARK ONE

MIRANDUS

SVARTURKUST

RAUTAKUST

IRON COAST

DE

DARKWALL

QUILTLANDS

ALFAJKUST

DAWN COAST

THE SENTINELS

THE KINGDOMS OF LIG

VITUS KIRKAS

BRIGHTHOME

S

MOD ISILW

HIGHGUARD

ULS KARKUN

THE RUST BANKS

DRULLKRETCH FOREST

PITCH

THE BLACKENED LANDS

DRAEKEN FORGE

THE ___TIAN ___TION

THE BACKFLOW

MALMAHAN'S FOLLY

SPECTRE'S WATCH

THE WARFIELDS OF KARKUN

PLAINS OF THRIST

QUIET RIVER

SHIELDREACH

___WOOD

ULS YDIN

PROLOGUE
THE HEART OF THE CITY

MIRANDUS.
THE BLACK CITY.
NOW.

GOOD DOES NOT EXIST, RASTIK.

TRY TO REMEMBER THAT. NOW MORE THAN EVER. HOLD IT IN YOUR MIND.

I KNOW, LORD.

THEY BROUGHT THIS ON THEMSELVES.

SHE MOST OF ALL.

NO, RASTIK. CLEAR YOUR THOUGHTS OF HATE OR THE BOND WILL BE CORRUPTED.

THIS IS MY CHOICE.

YOUR GRACE... IF THIS POOR DRULL COULD BE SO BOLD. THE CHOICE IS *OURS*.

YES. OF COURSE. YOU'RE RIGHT AS EVER, RASTIK.

MY THOUGHTS ARE ONLY OF THE DARK ONE. UNTIL *THE LIGHT* TAKES US.

THE UNSAFE BOY

YOU WANNA LET ME IN ON THE MYSTERY, PAUL?

YOU'RE ONLY SEVENTEEN, AFTER ALL. MOVING OUT IS A BIG STEP.

EARTH.
NEW YORK CITY.
THREE WEEKS AGO.

IT NEEDED TO HAPPEN. I JUST--I DIDN'T WANT TO BE THERE ANYMORE. SO WE MADE A DEAL. MOM'S FAMOUS FOR THEM.

I GET MY OWN PLACE. SHE GETS...

YOU ON THIS COUCH.

...TO TELL HER RICH FRIENDS I'M NOT *TOTALLY* CRAZY.

AND ARE YOU *ENJOYING* IT? LIVING ALONE?

I... SURE.

I'D LOVE TO KNOW SOME DETAILS.

WHAT'S TO SAY? I'M ALONE. THAT'S IT. JUST ME AND MY THOUGHTS AND SOME VERY LOCKED DOORS.

I DON'T HAVE TO BE CLOSE TO ANYONE AND NO ONE HAS TO BE CLOSE TO ME.

...

NO ONE GETS HURT.

ARE YOU DREAMING AT ALL?

NO.

...

YOU DON'T REMEMBER *ANYTHING* FROM WHEN YOU'RE ASLEEP?

NO. SLEEP'S NOT THE PROBLEM.

YOU SHOULD TELL HIM SOMETHING. TELL HIM JUST A LITTLE OF IT.

I CAN'T.

CAN'T WHAT?

...REMEMBER. MY DREAMS, I MEAN.

I WISH I COULD. DREAMING...

IT SOUNDS NICE.

I'D LIKE TO REVISIT YOUR CONCERNS THAT PEOPLE AREN'T *SAFE* AROUND YOU.

...

YOU CAN TELL HIM, PAUL. HE WANTS TO HELP. WE CAN LET HIM TRY.

THEY'RE NOT.

THAT'S A STRONG STATEMENT.

SOMETIMES, MY VISION GOES. JUST ON THE EDGES. GETS...*RED.* AND THERE'S A PRESSURE ON MY CHEST-- *IN* MY CHEST?

I FEEL LIKE I'M ABOUT TO UNRAVEL. NOT *SWEATER* UNRAVEL. LIKE...HIGH TENSION STEEL CABLE UNRAVEL. LIKE *COILS* OF ME ARE GOING TO *TEAR* THROUGH A FULL ROOM, AND PEOPLE...

PWEE~ PWEE~

TAKE YOUR TIME.

...PEOPLE ARE GOING TO *DIE*, DR. MARCUS.

PAUL.

ARE YOU CONSIDERING, OR HAVE YOU EVER CONSIDERED, HARMING EITHER YOURSELF OR OTHERS?

NO. THAT'S WHAT *I* DON'T WANT.

GOOD. THAT'S GOOD. YOU'RE A *UNIQUE* PATIENT, PAUL.

WE'VE KNOWN THIS SINCE YOU PROVED YOURSELF TO BE THE ONLY SOUL ON EARTH THAT LEONARD DOESN'T LIKE.

HSSSS

WHAT YOU'RE TELLING ME, IT'S GOOD.

YOU'RE SEEING SOMETHING IN YOURSELF, SOMETHING THAT *SCARES* YOU. BUT THAT FEAR COMES FROM WHAT MAY HAPPEN TO *OTHERS.*

I REALIZE IT'S A THIN SILVER LINING, BUT YOU'RE THINKING ABOUT SOMETHING-- *SOMEONE*-- BEYOND YOURSELF.

AND THAT'S... GOOD?

WELL, IT MEANS YOU'RE NOT A *SOCIOPATH.*

WAIT, DID YOU THINK I COULD BE A SOCIOPATH?

OF COURSE NOT, PAUL. BUT *YOU* DID.

THE HEAVY CHEST, BLINKY RED LIGHT? THAT'S A PANIC ATTACK. I WANT TO INCREASE YOUR NORMAL DOSAGE BY ANOTHER HALF PILL-- JUST SNAP 'EM WITH YOUR FINGER.

THIS WEEK, WHEN YOU GET SCARED. OR FEEL UNSAFE. OR LIKE YOU'RE ABOUT TO UNRAVEL.

TAKE A BREATH AND REMEMBER THAT *YOU* ARE YOUR ONLY CONCERN.

CARING ABOUT OTHER PEOPLE IS GREAT, BUT YOU, PAUL, ARE ALL YOU NEED TO WORRY ABOUT.

"YOU KNOW, FOR ONCE, I LOVE HIS ADVICE."

NO. NEVER.

MAYBE.

WOW, SO DECISIVE.

I DON'T KNOW, NIKKA! IT'S COMPLICATED! HOW WOULD I EVEN START?

SOMETHING LIKE, "DR. MARCUS, SOMETIMES I SEE AN ALIEN WORLD OF EVIL TWISTED DARK CRUEL MYSTERIOUS WEIRDNESS--"

STOP.

AND ALSO, I WANT TO RIP THE HEADS OFF MY CLASSMATES AND ANIMALS AND BURN THE WORLD TO THE--

STOP!

FINE.

BUT YOU SHOULDN'T LET THIS STUFF FESTER, MY DUDE. YOU'VE GOT TO LET IT OUT.

YOU DON'T KNOW WHAT YOU'RE SAYING. YOU DON'T KNOW WHAT WOULD HAPPEN.

I'M YOUR SISTER, PAUL. WHATEVER DOES HAPPEN, YOU CAN'T SCARE ME AWAY.

I DON'T HAVE A SISTER.

I NEVER DID.

THEN HOW DO YOU EXPLAIN THIS ADORABLE FACE!

YOU ARE SUCH A WEIRDO.

BUT YOU'RE MY WEIRDO. I GUESS.

HOW DID I GET SO LUCKY?

CLICK

CLACK

CLUNK

LAW & SONS
ALLOY COMPANY LTD

THE HEART OF THE CITY

find flaw
fix flaw
make other people
happy

NEW GAME DESIGN? BOARD OR VIDEO?

COMPUTER. I MEAN, EVENTUALLY. RIGHT NOW IT'S JUST A PAPER PROTOTYPE.

WANNA TALK IT THROUGH?

SNAP

...WRITE WHAT YOU KNOW.

OKAY, PAUL.

DEEP BREATH.

BEEP

HEY, MOM.

LAW
ALLOY CO

HOW WAS DR. MARCUS?

HE WAS GOOD, MOM.

BEST IN THE CITY, I HAVE IT ON GOOD AUTHORITY.

YEAH, FEELING MORE SANE ALREADY.

HOW WAS COURT?

BIGGEST CASE OF THE YEAR SO FAR.

NOT GUILTY. THAT MEANS A NICE BONUS, SO IF YOU NEED MONEY--

I DON'T.

HI, TREBOR!

YOU KNOW I WISH YOU'D LET ME HELP. I SPEND ALL DAY HELPING THE WORST PEOPLE IN THIS CITY, GIVING YOU A LITTLE SCRATCH IS THE LEAST--

MOM. CAN WE NOT DO THE MONEY THING?

WHATEVER YOU SAY. IT'S YOUR SPECIAL DAY, AFTER ALL.

HAPPY BIRTHDAY, PAUL.

BEEP

11 12
9 10
7 8

OH, MAN. DID SHE DO IT AGAIN?

MOM. MY BIRTHDAY'S NEXT WEEK.

BUT...I THOUGHT...

IT'S OKAY.

I ALWAYS SCREW THAT UP. I'M...

I'M SORRY, MOUSE.

IT'S...

IT'S OKAY, MOM.

REALLY. LET'S CHANGE THE SUBJECT.

YOU KNOW WHAT TO DO. ASK ABOUT WORK.

WHAT'S THE NEXT CASE?

BIG ONE. SERIAL KILLER... ALLEGEDLY.

YOU'RE DEFENDING A KILLER?

THAT'S THE JOB, SWEETIE.

LOVE THE UNLOVABLE.

OKAY, MOUSE. GOTTA GO. SAY HI TO YOUR...

MOM?

...NOTHING. NEVER MIND. THAT WAS WEIRD. FOR A MOMENT, I THOUGHT...

IT'S OKAY, MOM. LOT ON YOUR PLATE. UH, TALK TO YOU SOON.

SOUNDS GOOD. LOVE YOU.

≥SIGH≤

ONCE MORE UNTO THE BREACH.

BEEP

MARCY, I NEED THE FILES ON COLEMAN STEWART.

CAN YOU BRING UP THE CITY RECORDS? I CAN'T FIND THE REPORT.

WE FINISHED THAT ONE, REMEMBER?

OH SHOOT, THERE SHE IS.

YOUR COFFEE.

THANKS, REBECCA.

CONGRATS ON THE VERDICT. BET YOU'RE HAPPY ABOUT THAT BONUS.

YOU KNOW ME. IT'S ALL ABOUT THE WIN.

AND MS. YANG-TANASIN? MR. MITCHELL'S IN YOUR--

I SEE.

THAT'LL BE ALL, REBECCA.

CONGRATULATIONS, LIN.

TOLD YOU I'D GET THE ACQUITTAL, GEOFF.

LIKE I'D EVER DOUBT YOU. HOW'S PAUL?

LIVING IN A FLOP-HOUSE AND PRETENDING HIS THERAPIST IS HELPING. I FORGOT HIS BIRTHDAY AGAIN.

I SCREWED UP MARY'S ANNIVERSARY GIFT LAST YEAR. YOU MAY BE THE BEST DEFENSE LAWYER IN NEW YORK STATE, BUT YOU'RE STILL HUMAN.

WE'VE KNOWN EACH OTHER TWENTY YEARS. YOU REALLY AMBUSHED ME IN MY OFFICE TO GIVE ME A *PEP TALK?*

THEY MOVED UP THE HEARING.

REBECCA DIDN'T SAY ANYTHING.

NYPD CONTACTED THE PARTNERS DIRECTLY. APPARENTLY, THE MAN'S READY TO TALK AND KEEPS THREATENING TO GO QUIET UNLESS WE MOVE NOW.

NO REST FOR THE WICKED.

TRUE STORY. AND NEVER TRUER THAN NOW. I'D GET COMFY IF I WERE YOU, THIS IS GONNA TAKE THE REST OF THE DAY.

LET'S REVIEW THE STRANGE CASE OF *MISTER CALIGO.*

INTERESTING...

IT'S ALL CIRCUMSTANTIAL. HE HAS NO PRIORS, AND HIS TOXICOLOGY'S CLEAN.

FIFTEEN MURDERS, LIN.

WE'RE IN NEW YORK. FIFTEEN PEOPLE IS A BAD WEDNESDAY.

FACT IS, THERE'S NOT MUCH TO SAY THIS POOR GUY DID IT EXCEPT THE WORD OF A DETECTIVE AND SOME TRUE CRIME *PODCAST* INVESTIGATION INFLATING THE CIRCUMSTANTIAL EVIDENCE.

BUT POLICE TESTIMONY AND PUBLIC OPINION AREN'T SMALL HURDLES. AND THEY HAVE EYEWITNESSES.

YOU MEAN THE WITNESSES WHO CLAIM TO HAVE *FORGOTTEN* ABOUT THE MURDERS FOR A FEW YEARS UNTIL IT WAS CONVENIENT TO COME FORWARD? I THINK THEY'RE SUPPLYING US A LAUNDRY LIST OF POTENTIAL SUSPECTS WITH NO ALIBI.

LIKE, WHO *FORGETS* WATCHING A VICTIM GET THEIR NAILS TORN OFF ONE BY ONE? THAT'S INSANE. I DON'T BELIEVE IT FOR A MOMENT, AND NEITHER WILL A JURY.

YOU SHOULD TAKE THE PLEA.

NO. I CAN *WIN* THIS.

SO HERE'S WHERE I DELIVER THE BAD NEWS.

THE PARTNERS *WANT* A PLEA.

WHAT? DID YOU HEAR A *WORD* I JUST SAID? WE CAN GET THIS GUY OFF!

I BELIEVE YOU, LIN, BUT THE OTHERS DON'T WANT A WAR WITH THE GOVERNOR ON AN OFF-CYCLE YEAR.

MAKE A PLEA DEAL AND EVERYONE'S HAPPY.

...

OKAY. FINE. WHATEVER.

I KNOW IT'S HARD, BUT THEY'LL APPRECIATE YOU FOR IT. PARTNER'S ON THE TABLE.

ZORAN WOULD BE PROUD OF THE LION YOU'VE BECOME.

CALL ME WHEN YOU HAVE THE PLEA DEAL IN HAND.

SURE...AND GEOFF? LEAVE ZORAN OUT OF THIS.

IF YOU *INSIST.*

THRUNK

CLK THISH

PLUNK

AS LIGHT UNLOCKS THE FUTURE...

...LET WORLDS UNLOCK TO ME.

YOU MAY ANNOUNCE ME.

OF COURSE, THOU MOST WHITE.

ANNOUNCING!

THE ARCANE SHIELD OF MIRANDUS! THE DARK ONE'S BANE!

THE DESTINED ONE OF LIGHT'S KINGDOMS! THE HERO OF THE BURNING NIGHT! THE WHITE WIZARD...

ILLARION.

MY WHITE WIZARD.

GOSOVIC.

MY CHRONICLE KING.

GIVE US THE ROOM. ALL OF YOU.

I WILL STAY.

VERY WELL, FEOTORA. BUT I'LL HAVE SILENCE, EVEN FROM MY DAUGHTER.

WHAT NEWS I BRING IS DARK IN TIDINGS. IT CONCERNS THE BLACKENED LANDS AND THE DRULL BEYOND. OUR FRIENDS MAY BE THE WISER TO WALK AWAY FROM ITS HEARING.

THEN CALL ME A FOOL, ILLARION, FOR I WILL NOT CHOOSE WILLFUL IGNORANCE.

BRING ON YOUR STORM CLOUDS, MY WIZARD OF ILL TIDINGS.

I HAVE SEEN *THE DARK ONE.*

HRM

SNIFF

KRK

SNAP

YOU'RE CERTAIN?

I AM.

AND I'M SORRY.

ILLARION, APOLOGIES AREN'T NECESSARY. NOT NOW.

THE NARRATIVE ALWAYS STARTS ANOTHER VERSE.

WE REMAIN BUT MOMENTS IN ITS THRALL.

THIS IS OUR CHANCE, FATHER. I'LL BEGIN THE LONG HUNT, THE CULLING OF THE DRULL. MY MOST LOYAL CAN RIDE BY MORNING.

SEE THAT IT'S DONE.

AND I'LL BRING YOU HIS *HEAD*.

YOU WILL *HUNT HIS FOLLOWERS*. YOU WILL *DIMINISH HIS RANKS* BEFORE HIS *RISE*. BUT DAUGHTER, REMEMBER WELL WHO YOU ARE...

...AND WHO YOU ARE *NOT*.

IF THE DARK ONE RISES, THE *DESTINED ONE* WILL FOLLOW.

YOUR APPRENTICE IS READY?

SOON, MY LIEGE. THE BOY KRAISIS IS NEARLY A MAN. BUT THIS MAY REVEAL A HERETO-FORE UNFORSEEN *ADVANTAGE*.

WHAT UNFOLDS NOW IS *UNPRECEDENTED*. THE DARK ONE I HAVE SEEN... HE HAS NOT YET COME INTO HIS POWER.

FOR THE *FIRST* TIME IN THE NARRATIVE'S MANY CYCLES, WE HAVE THE CHANCE TO STAMP OUT THIS EVIL *BEFORE* ITS SURGE.

AN ENTIRE GENERATION CAN BE PROTECTED FROM THE BLOODSHED THAT WE KNOW TOO WELL.

BUT TO KILL THE DARK ONE BEFORE HE GAINS HIS POWER...

OUR NEW DESTINED ONE WOULD NOT RISE.

ALL YOUR PREPARATION OF THAT BOY, WHOM YOU SO FIRMLY BELIEVE WILL *REPLACE* YOU...IT WOULD BE FOR NOTHING.

I AM YOUR DESTINED ONE, MY KING.

NOTHING I DO IS FOR NOTHING.

WE ARE NOT YOUNG MEN, ILLARION. THIS IS A QUESTION OF GENERATIONS.

OUR CHAPTERS END. THE NARRATIVE DOES NOT.

SO YOU WOULD *CONDEMN* THE KINGDOMS OF LIGHT OUT OF MISPLACED MORALITY.

I WILL NOT COMMIT *MURDER* IN THE NAME OF *FEAR*. THE KINGDOMS OF LIGHT ARE THE STRONGEST THEY HAVE BEEN IN A CENTURY.

IT IS TIME FOR US TO BE HEROES, ILLARION, AS YOU WERE IN THE DAYS BEFORE. NOT ASSASSINS.

AND THAT IS THE END OF IT.

DUST TO BONE, LIFE OF ASH, SHATTERED SOUL, CUT BY GLASS.

IS THE INCURSION PREPARED, KRAISIS?

PFPFPFP

YES, ILLARION. THE *SIGIL OF SEEKING* HAS BEEN PLACED. THE DOORWAY, *DRAWN.*

AND OUR AGENT?

THIS MAN IS UTTERLY LOYAL TO THE KINGDOMS. CHAMPION OF SIX DUELS.

YOU KNOW YOUR ORDERS, KNIGHT?

BY YOUR POWER, I WILL KNOW THE DARK ONE. AND BY YOUR POWER, DESTINED ONE, I WILL SLAY HIM.

IN YOUR GLORY, ILLARION, WE ALL SHALL SHINE.

INDEED.

SNAP

GO FORTH, MY GOOD KNIGHT, INTO THE REALM BEYOND THE NARRATIVE'S KEN...

TIK

TAP

COUGH

PFSSH

NO...

YOU'RE JUST PANICKING. IT'S NOT REAL...

CALM DOWN...

CAFE

YOU CAN'T IGNORE IT, PAUL.

WHAT'S WRONG WITH ME?

IT'S NOT YOU THAT'S WRONG, PAUL. IT'S EVERYTHING ELSE. THIS WHOLE PLACE.

IT'S THIS REALITY, PAUL.

YOU DON'T BELONG HERE.

SHUT UP.

COULDN'T IF I WANTED TO.

WHY? WHAT THE HELL IS GOING ON?

DON'T CALL DR. MARCUS, PAUL. HE CAN'T HELP THIS.

...

DON'T DO IT. PLEASE.

IT'S COMING.

NOT THAT I'M COMPLAINING, PAUL, SINCE I'M A BIG ADVOCATE FOR SELF-CARE, BUT I DON'T USUALLY SEE THE SAME CLIENT TWICE IN A SINGLE DAY.

LET ALONE FOR AN EMERGENCY LATE NIGHT SESSION.

YOU WANNA TELL ME WHY YOU'RE HERE?

I HAD...A PROBLEM. AT A COFFEE SHOP. I SAW...THINGS.

IT'S GETTING CLOSER.

WHAT KIND OF THINGS, PAUL?

I...I HAVEN'T BEEN COMPLETELY HONEST WITH YOU, DOC. ABOUT MY... CONDITION.

MY, UM, RELATIONSHIP WITH REALITY IS...STRAINED. LIKE, WHAT DO YOU SEE WHEN YOU LOOK OUT THAT WINDOW?

I SEE RED HOOK. STREETLIGHTS. THE NEW YORK SKYLINE.

I SEE TWISTED TOWERS. LIGHTNING COMING OUT OF THE GROUND. AND...

AND WHAT, PAUL?

I'M SORRY, NIKKA.

I SEE A GIRL.

I SEE HER ALL THE TIME. HER NAME IS NIKKA. SHE SAYS SHE'S MY SISTER.

BUT I NEVER HAD A SISTER.

THAT WAS A MEAN THING TO SAY, PAUL.

AND HERE I WAS TRYING TO WARN YOU.

THIS GIRL. DOES SHE TELL YOU WHAT TO DO?

NO.

RUN, PAUL.

SHE *DOESN'T* TELL ME WHAT TO DO.

LISTEN TO ME. PLEASE.

YOU GOTTA *LEAVE.* RIGHT OUT THE WINDOW IF YOU HAVE TO.

IS SHE...

IS SHE HERE RIGHT NOW?

...

YES.

PAUL, *RUN!!* IT'S *SO* CLOSE!!

NO! I'M TIRED OF LIVING MY LIFE LIKE A *FREAK!* I'M NOT HIDING ANYMORE, I'M NOT DOING WHAT YOU SAY, I'M GOING TO GET *BETTER.* DO YOU HEAR ME?

YOU'RE NOT REAL! THAT WORLD ISN'T REAL!

NONE OF IT IS--

THUNK

SLNNG

TO PRESERVE THE LIGHT...

THE NARRATIVE IS SERVED.

THE PROPHECY IS FED WITH BLOOD.

YOU'RE NOT...YOU'RE NOT REAL--

HEY--

YOU READY TO LISTEN YET?

AAAHHH!

THWAM

GOOD. NOW GET UP. NO MATTER HOW MUCH IT HURTS.

AND FREAKING *RUN* ALREADY.

WHO...*WAS...THAT?!* WHAT'S *HAPPENING?!*

BELIEVE IT OR NOT, I'M ONLY SLIGHTLY LESS IN THE DARK THAN YOU.

WHAT DOES THAT EVEN MEAN?

THAT BIG GUY, I FELT HIM COMING, I WAS TRYING TO WARN YOU. MY HEAD IS CLOUDY BUT IT'S GETTING CLEARER BY THE MINUTE.

WHATEVER HE IS, I THINK WE'RE FROM THE SAME PLACE.

THE SAME *PLACE?!*

REMEMBER WHAT I SAID ABOUT REALITY? YOU'RE NOT CRAZY, PAUL. YOU JUST GOTTA REMEMBER.

I...OH NO...NO NO NO... DR. MARCUS.

I... NEED...TO BREATHE...

PAUL.

CLIP
CLOP
CLIP
CLOP

PAUL TANASIN OF EARTH.

HOW DO YOU KNOW MY NAME?

I AM SIR YSLA OF THE CHOSEN GUARD, FIRST OF MY RANK AND GLORIOUS AMONG ALL CRUSADERS.

IN THE NAME OF THE CHRONICLE KING AND HIS WHITE WIZARD ILLARION, DESTINED ONE OF LIGHT...

YOU ARE SENTENCED TO DIE.

PLEASE! I DON'T UNDERSTAND, PLEASE *STOP*--

STOP! CAN'T YOU HEAR ME?

I HAVEN'T *DONE* ANYTHING!

YOU *WOULD* HAVE...

SHREEEE

...BUT FOR THE WHITE WIZARD.

TINK

PAUL, YOU HAVE TO STOP HIM! IT *HURTS!*

PAUL?

VRRRM

WOW.

THAT WAS INSANE. I MEAN, THAT WAS *NUTS.* I MEAN, SHOOT, TRYING NOT TO BE INSENSITIVE HERE.

THAT WAS *EXTREMELY COOL.*

WHAT DID I...I JUST HEARD YOU SCREAMING...AND I SAW THAT IF...I COULD STOP HIM IF I REACHED OUT AND...

AND YOU *DID.* THAT WAS INCREDIBLE, PAUL...

YOU JUST KILLED A GUY FOR ME.

WAIT, NO, THAT DIDN'T SOUND GOOD. TRY AGAIN, NIKKA.

YOU JUST STOPPED AN *ASSASSIN*-- WITH MAGIC.

INTERMISSION

THE FIRST STORY TOLD

AND HOW AM I...HERE? THIS IS--

NIKKA, THIS IS MY *DREAM.*

YOU'RE SO CLOSE.

UNLESS...

IT'S NOT.

SNORF

HORMPH.

OKAY. NOT A DREAM.

THIS IS THE WRONG DAY TO COME AT ME, BIG UGLY.

I'M GONNA BE THE *WORST TOOTHPICK YOU EVER ATE.*

THRUM

THAT'S RIGHT, BIG GUY. PAUL TANASIN IS *NOT FOOD.*

HUROWz!

AND YOU'RE NOT *ALL THAT* UGLY.

HRMPH.

IT WOULDN'T BE MY FIRST ONE TODAY.

ONLY A FOOL *WANTS* A FIGHT.

SO.

WHICH ONE OF US IS A FOOL, THEN?

YOU'RE THE ONE RIDING AN *EVERMOUTH.* BE AWARE IT WILL SWALLOW YOU AT THE EARLIEST OPPORTUNITY. AND THEN IT WILL DIGEST YOU FOR THE REST OF YOUR LIFESPAN.

WHAT DO I CALL YOU, STRANGER?

THEN I SUGGEST YOU FOLLOW ME *OUT.*

I'M...

I'M PAUL.

AND I AM FEOTORA. THIRD OF MY NAME. PRINCESS OF LIGHT TO YOUR CHRONICLE KING GOSOVIC, WHO IS MY HONORED FATHER AND YOUR LIEGE AS A CITIZEN OF THE KINGDOM.

NOW, YOU SAY YOU'RE NOT OF THIS CURSED REALM?

HOW MANY SEASONS HAVE YOU STUDIED WITH THAT BLADE?

UM...WOULD YOU BELIEVE I GOT IT, LIKE, YESTERDAY?

YOU ARE TERRIBLE AT JOKES, PAUL THE FOOL, AND SHOULD REALLY STOP TRYING TO TELL THEM.

HISSSSS

HEY, CALM DOWN, BUDDY, IT'S OKAY, YOU'RE OKAY--

YOUR MOUNT IS A TRAITOR. HE CALLED THEM TO US.

IT'S ONLY RIGHT THAT HE BE THE FIRST TO DIE.

WHAT THE HELL, LADY? YOU DO KNOW THERE ARE WAYS TO SOLVE THINGS *WITHOUT VIOLENCE?*

I TOLD YOU, PAUL.

I'M NOT A LADY.

PAUL, *BEHIND YOU!!*

"LIN YANG-TANASIN, I'M FROM THE LAW FIRM OF MITCHELL AND YOUNG."

"I'M HERE TO SEE MY CLIENT."

COURSE.

PHOTO ID.

PRISONER NAME?

CALIGO.

SOLITARY'S ON THE LEFT.

NOBODY MENTIONED *THAT*.

NOT MY DECISION.

ON THE LEFT.

BZZZZ

FOR YOUR OWN PROTECTION, COUNSEL, YOU MUST OBSERVE THE FOLLOWING SECURITY PROTOCOLS DURING YOUR MEETING WITH THE PRISONER.

JUST LIN, PLEASE. MS. IF YOU HAVE TO, BUT I'M NOT MARRIED.

...OF COURSE YOU'RE NOT. MY MISTAKE.

YOU WANNA CLUE ME IN ON WHAT'S HAPPENING HERE? WHY THEY'RE TREATING YOU LIKE THIS?

A MAN SAID SOMETHING EXCEEDINGLY RACIST.

SO I BIT HIS TONGUE OUT.

GOOD THING I HAVE YOU. YOUR REPUTATION IS A TESTAMENT TO KEEPING PEOPLE LIKE ME AWAY FROM THE JUDGEMENT OF PRYING PEERS. I'D THINK *YOU'D* PREFER ME IN SOLITARY.

YOU'RE FAMILIAR WITH MY WORK?

OH.

I'M QUITE A FAN.

SO YOU KNOW MY REPUTATION, AND YET YOU'RE READY TO MAKE A DEAL? YOU'LL PLEA?

I DO. I AM. I WILL.

THIS NEXT ONE IS A HARD ASK, BUT IT'S MY JOB TO ASK IT.

TO HOW MANY OF THE MURDERS ARE YOU LOOKING TO PLEAD GUILTY?

ALL OF THEM. OBVIOUSLY.

EXCUSE ME, BUT I WANT TO MAKE SURE I GOT THAT RIGHT.

YOU WANT TO PLEAD GUILTY TO ALL FIFTEEN MURDER COUNTS?

MR. CALIGO, AS YOUR LAWYER, IT'S MY JOB TO INFORM YOU THAT A GUILTY PLEA OF THAT MAGNITUDE WON'T HELP US GET YOU FREE ON ANY KIND OF REASONABLE TIME--

FIFTEEN?

IS THAT ALL THEY FOUND?

MR. CALIGO...

...DO YOU HAVE INFORMATION ON OTHER MURDERS BEYOND THE SCOPE OF YOUR TRIAL?

BECAUSE IF WE CAN OFFER LAW ENFORCEMENT HELP IN SOLVING ANY CASE, NO MATTER HOW COLD, THEN YOU'RE LOOKING AT A MUCH MORE APPEALING PLEA DEAL.

IF I HELP THEM...WILL IT... WILL THEY...

MISTER CALIGO, I'M YOUR LAWYER.

WHATEVER IT IS YOU WANT, LET ME HELP YOU GET IT.

WHAT I WANT...

...IS FOR THE STATE TO KILL ME AS QUICKLY AS POSSIBLE.

THE STATE WANTS YOU IN FOR LIFE.

BUT WE HAVE A CHANCE TO GET YOU OUT IN TWENTY-- MAYBE FIFTEEN--IF WE REALLY TALK THIS THROUGH, CALMLY AND SANELY, AND WE GET A FAVORABLE PROSECUTOR.

BUT I'M NOT GOING TO SET YOU UP TO DIE.

YES, YOU ARE.

THAT'S MY REQUEST. IT'S YOUR JOB TO FOLLOW THROUGH.

I'LL CONSIDER YOUR... REQUEST.

BUT THIS RAISES A QUESTION, MR. CALIGO. ONE WE'LL NEED TO ANSWER.

IF YOU WANTED TO DIE SO BADLY, WHY NOT TAKE YOUR OWN LIFE BEFORE THEY CAUGHT UP WITH YOU? WHY GO TO ALL THIS TROUBLE WHEN YOU COULD'VE JUST...

WHAT CAN I SAY, *MRS.* TANASIN?

"...THAT'S JUST HOW IT WORKS."

CORRECTIONAL FACILITY

MAYBE FORTY-EIGHT HOURS.

WHAT'S AN HOUR?

NOW WHO'S TELLING WEIRD JOKES?

ABOUT WHAT?

THAT THING YOU JUST SAID...ABOUT HOURS.

YOU WERE, *UH*, JOKING. RIGHT?

YOU...

YOU REALLY DON'T KNOW WHAT AN HOUR IS?

AND YOU DON'T SEEM TO KNOW WHAT A *LIE* IS.

NOR HOW TO DISTINGUISH IT FROM A TRUTH TOLD TO SOMEONE TO WHOM YOU OWE FEALTY.

OR TO A FRIEND.

THE NARRATIVE IS EVERYWHERE.

NO MATTER WHERE YOU'RE FROM, IT'S WITH YOU NOW.

YOU'RE SAYING I WAS BROUGHT HERE. LIKE, BY SOMEONE?

NOT SOMEONE, PAUL. YOU WERE PULLED TO MIRANDUS BY THE INEVITABLE GRASP OF DESTINY. YOU HAVE A PLACE HERE, AS I DO. AS WE ALL DO.

EVEN THOSE DARK THINGS THAT WALK THIS CURSED LAND.

sniff sniff

IT'S THE NARRATIVE THAT BROUGHT YOU HERE, YOU WEIRD FOOL OF A BOY WITH A VERY POWERFUL SWORD. MAYBE YOU'RE MEANT TO PLAY A ROLE IN THE WAR TO COME.

CHOMP CHOMP

THERE'S A WAR COMING?

THE DARK ONE RISES. AND THE DESTINED ONE RISES TO CHALLENGE HIM.

AND THE DESTINED ONE WILL STAND VICTORIOUS.

THOSE AREN'T JUST WORDS. THEY ARE MY PEOPLE'S ENTIRE HISTORY. THEY ARE PROPHECY, AND THEY ARE OUR KEY TO THE PAST. IN MIRANDUS, THE NARRATIVE ALWAYS COMES TO PASS.

ALWAYS.

"THE DESTINED ONE IS THE NARRATIVE'S CHAMPION IN EACH GENERATION.

"ALTHOUGH MY FATHER, THE CHRONICLE KING, RULES THE KINGDOMS OF LIGHT AND SERVES AS VOICE TO THE NARRATIVE, HE IS BOUND TO MIRANDUS' SOIL.

"THE DESTINED ONE IS A GREAT HERO, RIGHTEOUS IN WORD, DEED, AND HEART. THEY CAN REACH TO WORLDS BEYOND BUT ARE BOUND TO MIRANDUS' VERY SOUL.

"THEIR MAGIC IS NOT A WEAPON, NO PALTRY TRICK OR DISTRACTION. IT IS TO WEAVE THE WORLD IN THEIR FAVOR.

"THE NARRATIVE WRITES ITSELF, BUT THE DESTINED ONE MAY EDIT THOSE WORDS TO AID THE LIGHT.

"AND THEY MUST WIELD THIS POWER WISELY, FOR THOUGH THEY ARE DESTINED TO LEAD MIRANDUS INTO A WORLD OF PURE LIGHT, THEY ARE ALWAYS OPPOSED...

CAN I TELL YOU SOMETHING SILLY, PAUL?

NOW THAT WE'RE BEING HONEST WITH EACH OTHER?

YEAH. COURSE. I MEAN, OF COURSE.

WHEN I WAS A LITTLE GIRL, I'D STEAL AWAY FROM THE CHRONICLE KEEP IN THE DEAD OF NIGHT TO FIND BRANCHES THAT FELL FROM THE GREAT TREE OF LIGHT.

I'D SHARPEN THEM WITH ROCKS AND TRAIN WHILE THE CITY SLEPT. I'D IMAGINE THE DRULL ARMIES BENEATH MY LITTLE BOOT. I'D IMAGINE THE DARK ONE'S HORRIBLE EYES AND HOW I'D CUT THEM OUT.

I KNEW, DEEP IN MY HEART, WHO I WAS. THE DESTINED ONE.

WHY IS THAT SILLY?

BECAUSE, PAUL.

I'M NOT.

THE WHITE WIZARD ILLARION, DESTINED ONE OF THE NARRATIVE PAST, SPEAKS WITH THE VOICE OF THE STORY. HE KNOWS WHO IT IS TO BE AND HAS BEEN GROOMING THE MAN SINCE HE WAS A BOY.

HIS APPRENTICE, KRAISIS. A MASTER OF SWORD AND SPELL. THE WHIM OF THE NARRATIVE MADE MANIFEST. HE'S NOT YET RISEN... BUT HE WILL.

THAT GIRL FIGHTING ON THE RAMPARTS WAS NOTHING BUT A WISH.

A DELUSION.

WHERE I COME FROM, THEY CALL ME DELUSIONAL, TOO, BUT--

CLNK

WHAT ARE YOU DOING?!

UH...HOLDING YOUR HAND? IN MY WORLD, IT'S A GESTURE OF...

WELL, IT MEANS WE'RE FRIENDS.

IN MY WORLD, IT MEANS YOU THINK I AM A CHILD, TO BE GUIDED THROUGH THE DARK. AS THOUGH I MIGHT WANDER OFF. AS THOUGH YOU ARE RESPONSIBLE FOR ME.

I AM RESPONSIBLE FOR *MYSELF*.

RIGHT. OF COURSE YOU ARE. I DIDN'T MEAN TO SUGGEST YOU WEREN'T.

YOU MIGHT BE THE MOST... *UH, RESPONSIBLE* PERSON I'VE EVER MET.

IN MIRANDUS, WE COVER THE NECK, FIRST. THIS SAYS, I WILL SUPPORT YOU, AND KEEP YOU CLOSE.

LIKE THIS?

YES. DO YOU FEEL MY PULSE?

I... I DO.

GOOD. I FEEL YOURS. OUR BLOOD BEATS TOGETHER.

THIS IS YOUR, *UM*... HANDSHAKE?

IT IS BETTER, YES?

...YEAH.

IT'S BETTER.

INTERMISSION

THE GARDEN OF STONE

I SAW HIM WITH MY OWN EYES! I WATCHED AS DRULL RAIDERS BOWED THEIR MALFORMED HEADS TO HIM, AS HE CONJURED THE POWER OF SOULS FROM THIN AIR!

HE WILL HAVE MADE CAMP IN PITCH BY NIGHTFALL. IT WILL TAKE HALF A MOON *MAYBE* FOR THE NECESSARY *SACRIFICES* TO BE MADE. HE WILL DRINK FROM THE WELL. ALL WILL RISE TO THEIR POSITIONS. AND UNLESS WE STRIKE NOW...

...HE WILL BE NEARLY UNSTOPPABLE.

NO DARK ONE IS UNSTOPPABLE.

NOT WHEN THE DESTINED ONE RISES.

SO OCCURS THE NARRATIVE.

SO OCCURS THE NARRATIVE!

AHEM.

MY LIEGE. LONG HAVE I PREDICTED THE RISE OF THE NEXT DESTINED ONE IN MY APPRENTICE *KRAISIS.*

MY KING.

IF WHAT THE PRINCESS SAYS IS TRUE, AND I'VE NO REASON TO DISBELIEVE HER, WE CANNOT WAIT FOR THE DESTINED ONE TO RISE.

WE MUST MAKE OUR *OWN* DESTINY.

EVER SINCE I MYSELF SERVED AS DESTINED ONE IN THE LAST TWO CYCLES OF THE NARRATIVE, ITSELF AN UNPRECEDENTED TENURE, THE RIVERS OF DESTINY HAVE PULLED ALONG THE YOUNG MAN AT MY SIDE. HE WILL BE THE ONE TO FOLLOW ME. HE WILL BE THE ONE TO RISE.

BUT IT IS NOT FOR YOU TO SAY.

YES, FATHER! KRAISIS MUST BE *ANOINTED* THE DESTINED ONE. WE *MUST* RIDE TO MEET THE DARK ONE BEFORE HE CAN TRULY COME INTO HIS POWER, LEST WE--

NO.

THE NARRATIVE RUNS ITS COURSE.

THOUGH TIME MOVES FORWARD, THE STORY IS UNCHANGING. IT IS PERFECT. IT HAS BEEN. IT ALWAYS WILL BE.

WE WAIT.

NO.

THE NARRATIVE LIVES, IT IS TRUE...

...BUT IT DOES NOT OPERATE ON OUR TIMELINE OR BY OUR WHIMS. AND THAT WHICH *BREAKS* IT CAN UNDO EVERYTHING WE HOLD DEAR.

SAYS THE *NARRATIVE.* AND, BECAUSE I AM ITS MOST *TRUSTED* SERVANT, THE ONLY DESTINED ONE IN HISTORY TO DEFEAT *TWO* DARK ONES...

YES, GOSOVIC.

HAVE YOU ALREADY FORGOTTEN THE INSTIGATOR MALMAHAN, THE ROGUE DARK ONE? THE ONE WHO ROSE WITH NO DESTINED ONE TO MATCH HIM AND NEARLY DESTROYED MIRANDUS?

HE WHO WAS ONLY STOPPED BECAUSE *I REFUSED TO WAIT?*

WE WILL NOT REPEAT THIS MISTAKE.

SAYS *YOU.*

SAYS *ME.*

NO.

THE DARK ONE RISES. AND THE DESTINED ONE RISES TO CHALLENGE HIM.

FATHER!

YOU ARE DISMISSED...

"...SO SAYS YOUR KING."

OH SH--

...

...DID YOU SEE THAT?

VERY MUCH, MY DARK LIEGE.

GREAT, I'M BEING TAILED BY A PEEPING GOBLIN.

GOBLINS ARE FROM STORIES. I AM *DRULL!*

I *DO NOT* CARE.

STOP FOLLOWING ME.

OF COURSE! I CAN STOP FOR...TEN BREATHS? PERHAPS FIFTEEN?

WHAT ABOUT ALL THE BREATHS?

I DON'T THINK HE'S GETTING IT.

AND I'M GONNA BE HONEST, "NICE" SEEMS LIKE A PRETTY RARE THING IN THIS PLACE.

THOUGH I COME FROM NEW YORK CITY SO, LIKE, MY STANDARDS ARE ALREADY LAX.

DON'T COME ANY CLOSER!

PAUL, IT'S ME--

I DON'T KNOW WHAT THE HELL YOU ARE, AND YOU KNOW IT.

STAY BACK.

HEY. IT'S OKAY.

YOU'RE SO CLOSE TO THE TRUTH NOW. YOU'RE ALMOST READY.

BUT RASTIK'S RIGHT...

YOU GOTTA DRINK.

IT WON'T JUST GIVE YOU POWER--THOUGH, DAMN IF IT'S NOT GONNA GIVE YOU A LOT OF THAT.

IT'LL ALSO GIVE YOU KNOWLEDGE. UNDERSTANDING. THE WATER DOWN THERE IS YOUR ONLY REAL PATH TO TRUTH.

IT'LL CHANGE YOU FOREVER, PAUL.

WHAT?

WHAT IF I DON'T WANT TO CHANGE?

NIKKA...

EVERY SINGLE DAY I LEFT MOM'S TOWNHOUSE, THERE WAS A HOMELESS GUY ON THE STOOP.

I THOUGHT HE WAS A FRIEND OF MOM'S, BEFORE I WAS OLD ENOUGH TO UNDERSTAND HOW THE WORLD WORKED.

SO I'D TALK TO HIM, RIGHT? THE WAY YOU DO WHEN YOU'RE A KID. WHEN EVERYONE'S FRIENDLY.

WHEN YOU DON'T KNOW BETTER.

AND HE'D ALWAYS BE FRIENDLY TO ME. FOR *YEARS*, I MEAN. A BIG SMILE. A WEIRD LITTLE QUIP. MAYBE JUST A GRUNT AS MOM DRAGGED ME PAST HIM.

BUT ONE MORNING...

...HE WAS JUST *SCREAMING*.

MOM TOLD ME HE'D "FALLEN OFF THE WAGON." THAT HE WASN'T HIMSELF ANYMORE.

THAT'S WHY HE WAS SCREAMING AT ME. THAT'S WHY HE TOLD AN ELEVEN-YEAR-OLD BOY THAT HE WAS GONNA POUND HIS FACE INTO THE PAVEMENT TILL THERE WAS NOTHING LEFT.

BUT *NOW*, I KNOW. IT WASN'T THAT HE'D MADE ONE BAD CHOICE ON ONE BAD NIGHT WHEN HE WAS FIFTY AND *THAT* MESSED UP HIS WHOLE LIFE.

IT'S THE DECISIONS HE MADE WHEN HE WAS *MY AGE*.

SOMEWHERE ALONG THE WAY, HE HAD A CHOICE. LET THE BEAST OUT OR CAGE IT.

PAUL, WHATEVER YOU THINK I AM--A FIGMENT, A DEMON, *WHATEVER*--WE CAN AT LEAST AGREE ON ONE THING, RIGHT?

I'VE KNOWN YOU YOUR WHOLE LIFE.

AND THAT WHOLE TIME, I'VE WATCHED YOU SHOVE PEOPLE OUT OF YOUR LIFE FASTER THAN THEY CAN GET IN.

MOM. FRIENDS. GIRLS.

YOU KNOW AS WELL AS I DO, THE ONLY REASON YOU KEPT *ME* AROUND WAS BECAUSE YOU DIDN'T HAVE A CHOICE.

POOR PAUL, A BULL FILLED WITH RAGE IN A WORLD MADE OF CHINA. LONELY PAUL, WHO HAD TO HIDE FOR FEAR HE'D WAKE UP HAVING MURDERED HIS FRIENDS. WEIRD PAUL, WHO NO ONE UNDERSTOOD.

ALL TO PROTECT THE FRAGILE LITTLE PEOPLE IN YOUR LIFE. THE ONES WHO COULD NEVER HOPE TO UNDERSTAND.

BUT IT'S YOU WHO NEVER UNDERSTOOD. AND I COULD NEVER *TELL* YOU WHAT I KNEW.

I WAS BOUND BY RULES. UNTIL WE CAME HERE. UNTIL WE WERE THIS CLOSE TO THE WELL.

WHAT DOES THAT MEAN?

IT MEANS I CAN FINALLY REMEMBER WHAT I AM. WHAT YOU'VE FORGOTTEN.

AND IT MEANS, SURROUNDED BY ALL THIS POWER, IN THIS PLACE...

I CAN SHOW YOU.

IN RETURN FOR THIS ADDITIONAL INFORMATION--FOR THE CLOSURE IT WILL BRING, FOR THE LIVES THAT WILL BEGIN TO HEAL-- MY CLIENT HAS ONE UNUSUAL REQUEST.

IF YOU WANT HIS COOPERATION, IT IS *NON-NEGOTIABLE.*

LUCKILY, IT IS ALSO SOMETHING THAT MANY OUTSIDE, AND *IN THIS ROOM,* SEEK. IT IS, *EVEN I BELIEVE,* WHAT MY CLIENT *DESERVES.*

MY CLIENT REQUESTS THE *DEATH PENALTY.*

MY CLIENT *WISHES TO DIE.*

DEFENSE. MY CHAMBERS. NOW.

CALIGO IS A MURDERER. HE... *IS.* THAT IS A FACT. BUT HE IS ALSO A HUMAN BEING. A HUMAN BEING WHO IS BEGGING TO BE RELEASED FROM HIS--

CUT IT, COUNSEL.

THE DEVIL GETS NO TEARS IN THIS CHAMBER.

FINE.

I LOVE MY JOB. I AM DAMN GOOD AT MY JOB. MARK THIS WITH A "W," AND I'M ALL BUT PARTNER.

BUT I SERVE *MY CLIENT.* AND THAT *ANIMAL* HAS DONE MORE EVIL TO THIS WORLD THAN WE CAN EVER KNOW.

YES, I WANT HIM TO BE LOCKED UP FOREVER, AND YES, I GENUINELY WANT CLOSURE FOR THOSE WHOM HE'S MADE SUFFER.

BUT I HAVE A DUTY TO THIS COURT THAT IS BIGGER THAN ME, OR MY FIRM. IT IS ABOUT THE NATURE OF LAW, AND THE RIGHT TO REPRESENTATION.

THEN RECUSE YOURSELF FROM THIS CASE.

ZORAN USED TO SAY SOMETHING TO ME. RIGHT BEFORE HE'D DO SOMETHING STUPID, OR DISAPPEAR...*AGAIN.* HE'D SAY, "EVERY MOMENT, ALL YOU CAN BE IS YOURSELF."

I CANNOT RUN FROM THIS CASE, YOUR HONOR. I AM CALIGO'S DEFENSE, AND I MUST *DEFEND.*

IT IS ALL I KNOW HOW TO BE.

KRAISIS!

APPRENTICE TO ILLARION!

DESTINED ONE WHO WOULD WAIT ON THE SIDELINES!

DO NOT YET DROP YOUR BLADE...

KLNK

I HAD HIM.

YOU DIDN'T. AND BEFORE YOU ASK ME HOW I *KNOW* YOU WERE ABOUT TO HAVE A FRACTURED SKULL AT THE HAND OF KRAISIS, LET ME REMIND YOU OF MY UNIQUE RELATIONSHIP WITH THE NARRATIVE.

I NEED NO REMINDING, ILLARION. MY STUDIES--

ARE WOEFULLY INCOMPLETE. THUS MY... *INTERVENTION*.

WHAT DO YOU MEAN, INCOMPLETE?

I MEAN EXACTLY THAT.

YOU KNOW WHAT YOUR FATHER'S BOOKS HAVE TAUGHT YOU, WHAT YOUR FATHER'S SCRIBES HAVE SHOWN YOU, WHAT YOUR FATHER'S SCHOLARS HAVE LECTURED YOU.

YOU KNOW WHAT YOUR FATHER WOULD *HAVE* YOU KNOW.

YOU'RE WISE TO NOTICE MY ANGER WITH KING GOSOVIC.

BUT THAT'S AS FAR AS IT GOES. ANGER.

NEVER TREACHERY.

NOR WOULD I EVER PREACH SUCH THINGS, PRINCESS. BUT LET ME ASSURE YOU...

...YOU HAVE REASON FOR ANGER. AND SO MUCH MORE.

FOR THERE IS MUCH YOU DO NOT KNOW.

BUT SECRETS ARE NOTHING TO THE LIGHT. SO PLEASE...

I THINK IT'S TIME I ENLIGHTENED YOU.

I CAN HEAR YOUR ARGUMENT NOW. THE NARRATIVE DOES AS IT WILL. CHANGING ITS WAYS WOULD BE HERESY.

IF YOU ALREADY KNOW WHAT I'M GOING TO SAY, WHY ARGUE?

BECAUSE WE'RE *ALREADY* COMMITTING HERESY AGAINST THE NARRATIVE.

ALL SO YOU CAN, WHAT? *FORCE* THE NARRATIVE TO ACCEPT YOUR PRECIOUS *KRAISIS* AS THE DESTINED ONE?

KRAISIS IS A SYMBOL, FEOTORA.

A MAN OF MIRANDUS ABLE TO PROTECT HIS PEOPLE FROM THE DARKNESS. WOULD YOU TRULY RATHER THAT DESTINY FALL ON SOME OUTSIDER LIKE THIS BOY *PAUL?*

I...

DOES MY FATHER KNOW?

NO. BUT I HAVE TRIED TO OPEN HIS MIND AND HE REFUSES TO SEE. HE'S PARALYZED BY THAT SAME INACTION YOU FEEL NOW.

THAT SAME DEEP DESIRE TO ALLOW THE NARRATIVE TO CONTINUE ON ITS COURSE, EVEN AS IT SATISFIES THE WHIMS OF A WORLD APART FROM YOUR OWN.

IT IS LIKE YOUR FIGHT WITH KRAISIS. YOU CANNOT WIN WITH RESILIENCE ALONE.

WE MUST FREE OURSELVES FROM THE INFLUENCE OF EARTH. THE PEOPLE MUST KNOW THE TRUTH. THEY MUST *WILL* THE NARRATIVE TO CHANGE, TO ELEVATE KRAISIS IN PLACE OF SOME CHILD.

I MUST BE THE LAST DESTINED ONE NOT OF MIRANDUS.

AND IT MUST BE A TRUE LEADER WHO BRINGS US THERE.

DO YOU UNDERSTAND WHAT I'M ASKING OF YOU, FEOTORA?

DO YOU KNOW THE HERO I AM ASKING YOU TO BE?

IF ONLY
YOU COULD SEE
THE TRUTH.

CLINK

"AWAKEN,
MY LOVE!"

THE EYES OF THE WORLD ARE ON US, LADIES AND GENTLEMEN.

WHAT HAPPENS IN THIS COURT IS MORE THAN US. IT IS WRITTEN INTO OUR HISTORY. WHICH BECOMES OUR FUTURE.

AND THAT FUTURE IS WHAT WE--ALL OF US--MUST LOOK TO. THE LEGACY WE LEAVE. THE STORY WE TELL.

THE COURT *DENIES* THE DEFENDANT'S REQUEST.

THE STATE OF NEW YORK DOES NOT, AND WILL NOT, ACCEPT *EXECUTION* AS AN ACCEPTABLE PUNISHMENT. EVEN FOR SOMEONE WHOSE CHARGES ARE AS SEVERE AS THOSE MR. CALIGO FACES.

THE CASE WILL CONTINUE *AS SCHEDULED.*

PAUL, THIS IS YOUR BABY SISTER. HER NAME IS *NIKKA*.

NIK-KA.

DADDY BACK?

WE SHOULD GO BACK TO SLEEP, NIKKA.

DAD'S OFFICE

PAUL, KEEP UP.

CAN I CAN I CAN I CAN I MOMMY *PLEASE!?*

OKAY, BABY, OKAY--

"...YOU WON'T REMEMBER HIM LONG.

"NONE OF YOU WILL.

DON'T YOU *DARE* STAY A DAY-- NOT EVEN A *DAY*-- LONGER THAN YOU HAVE TO.

I KEEP TELLING YOU, LIN...

THEY DON'T HAVE *DAYS* WHERE I'M GOING.

YER DOING IT!

YER *DOING IT!*

DID YOU HEAR ME, PAUL?

KEEP UP.

"I'M SO SORRY, LIN. I TRIED. WE ALL TRIED.

"IF IT'S ANY CONSOLATION...

WE GATHER HERE TODAY TO MOURN THE LOSS OF *ZORAN TANASIN.* FATHER, HUSBAND, FRIEND. TAKEN BEFORE HIS TIME.

WOULD ANYONE LIKE TO SAY ANY WORDS?

"AFTER TWO DAYS, WE COULDN'T REMEMBER HIS FACE.

"AFTER FOUR DAYS, HIS VOICE WAS GONE FOREVER.

WITHIN A WEEK, WE WOULD BARELY EVEN REMEMBER WE HAD A FATHER.

"BUT WE HAD EACH OTHER.

PSSST, NIKKA!

NIKKA!

"YOU KNEW HOW MUCH I'D ALWAYS WANTED TO GO IN DAD'S STUDY. ALMOST AS MUCH AS YOU DID.

"YOU'D BEEN PRACTICING FOR THE NEXT TIME HE WAS GONE.

'S OFFICE

C'MERE. QUICK!

DAD'S OFFICE

"YOU SAID IT WAS A PRESENT FOR ME, BUT I THINK WE BOTH KNOW YOU WOULD'VE GONE WITHOUT ME.

"JUST LIKE YOU SHOULD'VE."

"WE DIDN'T.

"ALL WE SAW WAS A WORLD FOR US.

"NO CORNER TO HIDE IN. NO BULLIES TO AVOID. NO PRYING EYES TO FEAR. NO TEARS FROM OUR MOTHER.

"JUST A WORLD THAT FELT OPEN AND ENDLESS, LIKE THE FIRST HOURS OF A SUNDAY MORNING.

"AND A STRANGER HIGH ABOVE SHOUTING A WORD WE DIDN'T HEAR UNTIL TOO LATE.

NIKKA...

I'M SORRY.

HONESTLY? TOO LATE FOR THAT.

I'VE WATCHED YOU EVERY DAY SINCE YOU TRAPPED ME IN THAT STUPID NECKLACE. I DON'T WANT YOU TO BE SORRY.

I WANT YOU TO BE YOU.

IT'S LIKE THEY SAY...

THE DARK ONE DRINKS FROM THE WELL...

AND ALL RISE TO THEIR POSITION.

INTERMISSION

THE TRAGEDIE OF THE BOY KARKUN

Act V. Scene 3.
THE WELL OF DARKNESS.

Enter KARKUN. At his feet, the bodies of his MOTHER
FATHER & KESSILE lye. A bloody scene.

KUN:

...n first I learn'd dark future's play
...s I not feared ~ both for myself and
...u, my mother? Father too and Kessile
...whose eyes could light this foulest place
...but now are e'er destroyed?

Was it not your council, Father, to be
thusly cautious of the bane Mirandus?
Was I not there hearing and receptive
to that wisdom? Did I not say "yes, father,
ne'er shall I cede life for destined doom"
and did you not comfort me?
Did I not after gaze into the eyes of Kessile
and kiss her softly in that way that makes me
sure I am a man,
...rk upon fate's wall of fools?

Aye. Aye to all. Yet still I stand...
knave and murdr'er all to serve
Mirandus, monster particoat in d...
Her tricks of destinie are iron cla...
upon my each intention, and e'er I t...
goodness, they will steer for ill.
Now all I know is gone to death.
I'd crie to God but he in mind inf...
cast aside my ear. And now it f...
naught but other worlds becko...
Now I step fatefully beyond
and all ties sev'red, invite n...

Karkun reaches into the

KARKUN:

It ought be pain o'erwhelm me now
Some secret sadness fear or lust
Some guilt perhaps to feel in this
my final breath as human man.
And yet...

I am relieved
of care as well as mortal coil.
So am I truly free.

The boy KARKUN howls.
He is as a wolf.
He SNARLS.

escap'd from expert monger,
perfect bait but we refuse the gift
lest chaos not be let to reign.

We call ourselves free men but
all we've been is chance's pawn
see that now. The dark bey
is not a curse nor hated
enemie but hymn to s
many verses in wh
might write my

Nay, who
And
alo

ckoning.

He DRINKS.

KARKUN:
Death! Death and woe and dark to
That which hides in Light! For
strength not righteous whim makes
right in truth!

We earthbound   rows kno
           all that No

William: this new
play Karkun is
naught but hogwash.
The King beseeches
you start another for
performance at the
Globe in one fortnig

y, the same young k
knew a moment just before.
ere's diff'rence, yes, but none so dear –
e burned only his soul from here
And carved his skull to fit my own
And yes, I've had his body grown
But he's the same, be not afright
A good man speaks to you tonight.

Kingdoms of the Light Defy'nt, lend an
ear to he who'd see you buried low
and be forgotten so that none might
know that es ever stood against
the dark.

Destined your One may st with
Armies mighty at command to
punish Drull~ Sweet Drull
to rend and

Though cloaked in blinding light you
stand I swear that though I fall so shall
I rise. Again, again! Infinite more!

Until I have Consum'd your will
to battle forth To Narrative's
bleak end.

A human child I'll take for mine
With mind atrouble, features fine
And woe be oft to he who bears me
On my final form, I dare thee
Look upon and know thy death
In time the dark consumes the rest!
Lo, though Karkun's a setting sun

One day I'll see my battle won

A NEW NARRATIVE

THE LIGHT HAS COME.

THE LIGHT HAS COME!

THE LIGHT! THE LIGHT!

DOOOOOM

KINGDOMS OF THE LIGHT DEFY'NT, LEND AN EAR TO HE WHO'D SEE YOU BURIED LOW...

WE ARE OUTNUMBERED.

INCREDIBLY SO.

THEN WE MUST ACTIVATE THE *IRON-KEEPERS*.

SADLY, MY LIEGE--

YES, I KNOW, IT IS *I* WHO MUST DO IT. WHICH MEANS EVEN MORE SACRIFICES. HOW MANY MUST DIE? TEN? ONE HUNDRED?

JUST *ONE*.

NO. BRING ME ANOTHER.

NONE IS SO TRAINED.

I DON'T CARE. THERE WILL BE SOME OTHER WAY TO DEFEAT FEOTORA AND HER HORDE. ANOTHER WAY THAT DOESN'T INVOLVE...

IN THE KINGDOMS OF LIGHT, THEY SAY THAT A DRULL LIFE IS SAD. IT IS VICIOUS AND SMALL. BLACKENED AND BURNT.

THEY DO NOT VISIT OUR DENS. THEY DO NOT GNASH WITH US. THEY DO NOT SEE THE *LIVING* THAT WE DO.

THEY DO NOT SEE THE WAY WE WORSHIP. THEY DO NOT SEE OUR FAITH.

A DRULL LIFE--*THIS* DRULL'S LIFE--IT ISN'T SAD.

IT IS *GOOD*, MY MASTER.

GOOD DOES NOT EXIST, RASTIK.

TRY TO REMEMBER THAT. NOW MORE THAN EVER. HOLD IT IN YOUR MIND.

I KNOW, LORD.

THEY BROUGHT THIS ON THEMSELVES.

SHE MOST OF ALL.

NO, RASTIK. CLEAR YOUR THOUGHTS OF HATE OR THE BOND WILL BE CORRUPTED.

THIS IS MY CHOICE.

YOUR GRACE... IF THIS POOR DRULL COULD BE SO BOLD. THE CHOICE IS *OURS.*

YES. OF COURSE. YOU'RE RIGHT AS EVER, RASTIK.

MY THOUGHTS ARE ONLY OF THE DARK ONE. UNTIL *THE LIGHT* TAKES US.

SHING

FOR!

THE!

SLICE

LIGHT...

GAHH!

FOOSH

IDIOT MONSTER!

I AM NOT ALL I HAVE TO WORRY ABOUT.

CLANG.

I AM BLESSED.

CHOSEN BY THE WHITE WIZARD, HIS POWER IS MINE.

I AM THE NARRATIVE'S WILL MADE FLESH!

I'M SIMPLY CHOOSING TO *LIVE!*

YOU KILLED KRAISIS. THE DESTINED ONE IS *DEAD.*

WHICH MEANS THIS FIGHT IS *OVER,* PRINCESS! PUT DOWN YOUR WEAPONS AND RETREAT.

OR PUT THEM DOWN... AND STAY.

I FELT YOUR PULSE. YOU FELT MINE.

...OUR BLOOD BEAT TOGETHER.

FEOTORA, THIRD OF HER NAME. ONLY A FOOL WANTS A FIGHT.

THEN I AM A FOOL.

TIME FOR SOMETHING NEW.

WHAT? NO--

NOOOOOOOO!

WE HAVE THE SUSPECT IN CUSTODY BUT NO EYES ON TANASIN.

DID YOU JUST SAY TANASIN?!

WHERE IS SHE?!

I DON'T UNDERSTAND WHAT'S HAPPENING!

LIN YANG-TANASIN, YOUR HOSTAGE! WHERE IS SHE?!

I DON'T KNOW--

THEN STAND UP. YOU'RE GOING OUTSIDE.

NO. I'M GOING WHERE I WANT.

AND THERE'S NOTHING YOU CAN DO TO STOP ME.

SUSPECT IS RESISTING ARREST!

I'M PUTTING HIM DOWN!

WAIT, NO--

EPILOGUE
PERAGATOR

"I THOUGHT IT WOULD BE ME."

END
BOOK ONE